PICK-A-PATH #1

The
Dandee Diamond
Mystery

by JANE O'CONNOR and JOYCE MILTON

illustrated by DARYL CAGLE

D0595705

SCHOLASTIC INC.
New York Toronto London Auckland Sydney

ISBN 0-590-32742-9

Text copyright © 1982 by Jane O'Connor and Joyce Milton. Illustrations copyright © 1982 by Scholastic Inc. All rights reserved. Published by Scholastic Inc.

12 11 10 9 8 7 6 5 4   3 4 5/9

Printed in the U.S.A.

40

The Dandee Diamond Mystery

READ THIS FIRST!

Your rich great-uncle has just died and left a very strange will. Someone is going to inherit the priceless Dandee Diamond . . . but *who???* And where is the diamond hidden???

You can solve the mystery! The answer depends on the decisions you make. Start reading on page 1 and read until you have a choice to make. Then decide what you want to do and turn to the page that goes with that choice. Keep following directions until you come to THE END.

If you don't like the way the mystery has turned out, don't worry. You can go back to page 1 and follow another trail of clues. Change your mind, and you can change the ending of the story. It is all up to you!

Your nutty uncle, Herbert J. Bone, the richest man in all of Bonesboro, has just died at the ripe old age of 93.

You are surprised to learn that you, who haven't seen Uncle Herbert since you were a baby, are invited to the reading of the will.

Three other people are waiting when you arrive at the library of Uncle Herbert's mansion. They are: your drippy cousin Roderick . . . Captain Jack Scull, your Uncle Herbert's closest friend . . . and Drusilla Devine, the famous movie actress who gave up her career to marry your uncle.

In walks Uncle Herbert's lawyer. He clears his throat and announces, "The will is very short. Here it is."

Turn to **page 2.**

Last Will and Testament

I, Herbert J. Bone of Bonesville in the County of Bones Bon and State of Bonestock, being of sound mind and memory, do make, publish and declare this my last Will and Testament, in manner following:

I am leaving my money to charity and my collection of rare bugs to Drusilla. I know you are all wondering who will get the fabulous 1000 carat Dandee Diamond. That will go to the one who deserves it most.

In Witness Whereof I have hereunto subscribed my name the fifth day of September in the year 1994

Herbert Bone L.S.

PS. If you want to know more,
ask my parrot, Arthur.

"Rare bugs, my foot!" sputters Drusilla. "*I* deserve that diamond."

You are not sure. If Uncle Herbert had wanted Drusilla to get the diamond, he would have left it to her by name. Like everyone else, you turn toward the parrot to see what he will say.

Go on to the next page.

"CHINA...CHINA," squawks Arthur, as if on cue. "LOOK IN CHINA . . ."

"China!"exclaims Captain Jack."That's where Herb got the diamond. He won it in a checkers game from that crazy archaeologist, Manfred Dandee. I bet the diamond is somewhere in China now."

"Don't be silly," says Aunt Drusilla in her most haughty voice. "I'm sure Herbert left it hidden in the famous Bone China Collection. He gave it to the Bonesboro Museum just last month."

Cousin Roderick says nothing. If he has any idea he isn't talking.

Drusilla calls her chauffeur. She is heading for the museum.

"Well," Captain Jack says, "looks like *I'll* be sailing for China tonight on my boat, the *Scull and Bones*. Anyone want to come along?"

If you want to go with Captain Jack, turn to **page 6.**

If you decide to follow Drusilla to the museum, turn to **page 4.**

4   You arrive at the Bonesboro Museum just after Drusilla. She leaps from her car, and you follow her inside past the Herbert J. Bone Dinosaur Bone Exhibit, the Bone Rare Bugs Room, and the H.J. Bone Gallery of Forgotten Painters.

Drusilla knows where she's going — straight to the Bone China Collection.

She marches over to the glass case that holds the biggest pieces of china. She takes off a shoe and smashes open the case.

"AHA!" she cries, reaching inside a large teapot. She pulls something out. But it is just a scrap of paper.

" 'What has feet but cannot walk?' " Drusilla reads, stamping her foot impatiently. "Oh, that Herbert! Not another one of his silly riddles!" Then she pauses. "But wait . . . the answer might be a piano. Herbert gave me a grand piano for a wedding present."

Go on to the next page.

Just then Roderick pops out from behind a mummy case. "A statue has feet but cannot walk," he pipes up. "I bet the diamond is in that statue of Uncle Herbert in the Bonesboro town square."

Who do you think has the best answer?
If you think Drusilla does,
turn to **page 8.**

If you think Roderick does,
turn to **page 18.**

6   You decide to go with Captain Jack. That night you set sail for China aboard the *Scull and Bones*.

"Ahhh!" bellows Captain Jack. "Nothing beats life on the high seas."

You are not so sure. Giant waves are slamming against the sides of the boat. A storm is blowing up.

You hear Captain Jack shouting.

"What?" you cry, as a wave smacks you in the face and knocks you down.

The *Scull and Bones* is in trouble. It is bouncing on the water like a toy boat. And where is Captain Jack? You can't see him anywhere!

What will you do now?
If you take a lifeboat and
try to head back to Bonesboro,
turn to **page 24.**

If you decide to stay
on board and help
Captain Jack,
turn to **page 10.**

8   You think the piano is a good place to look, so you follow Drusilla back to Uncle Herbert's house.

"The diamond has to be here," Drusilla snarls. She struggles to open the lid of the grand piano, but it is hard work with those long, dragon-lady fingernails of hers.

You try to help. But Drusilla wants no part of you. "Out of my way, buster," she snaps, shoving you aside.

Go on to the next page.

The piano lid opens — inside is a tape recorder!

Drusilla turns it on.

"Heh, heh, heh," Uncle Herbert's voice cackles. "You've struck a false note. There's no diamond in here."

Drusilla leaves in a fury.

Do you stay and keep looking for another clue? If so, turn to **page 12.**

Or, if you think you've reached a dead end and don't know what to do, turn to **page 52.**

10   You stay on the *Scull and Bones* and find Captain Jack. He is hurt! The tiller has swung around and knocked him unconscious.

After you take him below deck, you steer the boat through the storm all by yourself.

Much to your surprise, you are a pretty good sailor. For many days Captain Jack is too weak to do any work. But he tells you how to steer a course for China by following the stars. You even learn to tell port from starboard and to stop calling the galley "the kitchen."

"For a little landlubber, you're doing all right," Captain Jack tells you one day. "Old Herb would be proud."

Turn to **page 14.**

12   After Drusilla leaves, you pick up the tape recorder. Taped to the back is a piece of paper. It looks like another clue. That tricky Uncle Herbert!

You open the paper and read:

Good for you! You've made it this far. Now follow the maze.

Herbert J. Bone, Esquire

Find your way through the maze on the next page.

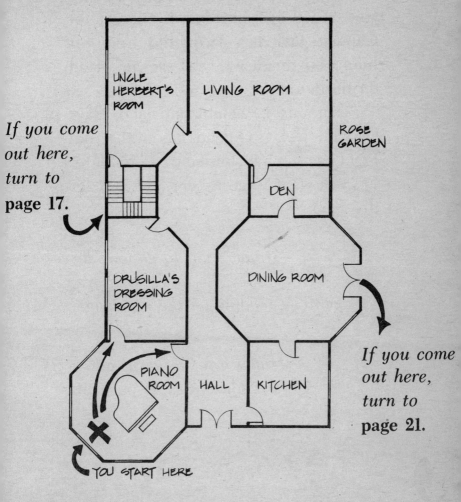

If you come out here, turn to page 17.

UNCLE HERBERT'S ROOM

LIVING ROOM

ROSE GARDEN

DEN

DRUSILLA'S DRESSING ROOM

DINING ROOM

PIANO ROOM

HALL

KITCHEN

If you come out here, turn to page 21.

YOU START HERE

14   For days you sail without spotting land. Then one morning, not long after Captain Jack has recovered from his bump on the head, you see an island on the horizon.

"That must be Doubloon Island," says Captain Jack. "Legend has it that old Peg Leg the Pirate buried treasure there. Do you want to go ashore and look for it?"

If you want to go look for the treasure, continue reading on the next page.

If you want to keep sailing for China, turn to **page 31.**

You decide you want to look for treasure on Doubloon Island.

"You take the lifeboat and go ashore," says Captain Jack. "I will wait here for you on the *Scull and Bones*."

Turn to **page 20.**

You go up to Arthur the parrot's room. Arthur is in his cage. It is the biggest bird cage you've ever seen, and it's made of solid gold.

"Squawk," says Arthur.

"Where is the diamond?" you ask.

"China . . . China . . . look in China," croaks Arthur.

You've heard that before! Arthur is in no hurry to help you solve the mystery. He flies over to his birdbath and begins splashing around in the water. Then you notice the words MADE IN CHINA printed on the side of the birdbath. Hmmmmmm!

Look — there is something sparkling in the water . . .

Turn to **page 29.**

You follow Roderick to the Bonesboro town square. He is not very happy to have you tagging along.

Standing on a pedestal carved with the motto "Money Is Nice" is an eight-foot statue of your four-foot-eleven-inch Uncle Herbert. At the same moment, you and Roderick spy an envelope in the statue's left hand. Roderick jumps up and down grabbing for the letter, but it is out of reach. Lucky for you, you've worn your Super-Sporto sneakers.

"Let me handle this," you say. You scramble up the statue and get the letter.

"That belongs to me," Roderick shouts up at you. "The statue was my idea!"

"Maybe so," you answer. "But now I have the letter."

Roderick thinks it over. "Okay, fair is fair," he says. "We'll be partners from now on."

You climb down and open the letter. You and Roderick read it together.

Turn to **page 22.**

As you reach the island, you see the *Scull and Bones* sail away.

"I'm shoving off, matey," you hear Captain Jack shout. "I'm bound for China, and the diamond will be mine . . . *all mine!*"

You can't believe your ears. After all you've done to help Captain Jack, he isn't a bit grateful!

It looks as if you are marooned on Doubloon Island.

Is this THE END?

No! Turn to **page 54.**

You go to the side entrance of the house. A long, shiny black car is waiting there. The driver is wearing a fancy uniform. He smiles and tells you to get inside.

"Where are you taking me?" you ask.

"You will soon find out," he says mysteriously.

Turn to **page 27.**

The letter says:

> You were pretty smart to think of
> the statue. But it's the wrong
> answer to my riddle.
> Think again. What else has feet
> but cannot walk?
> Give up? Okay, I'll tell you.
> It's a YARD — a yard has three
> feet in it.
> > Fooled you again,
> > Herbert J. Bone, Esquire

"A yard," groans Roderick. "What does Uncle Herbert mean by that?"

"Wait a minute," you say. "Didn't Uncle Herbert spend a lot of time in his *yard?* My mother always said he loved gardening."

Go on to the next page.

Roderick scratches his head. "That's not a bad idea."

Before you know what is happening, he runs to the corner bus stop and jumps aboard a waiting bus. You run after him. As the doors slam in your face you hear Roderick shout, "So long, sucker! You didn't really think I was going to share the diamond, did you?"

You are hitting yourself on the head for the fiftieth time when a long, shiny black car pulls up. The chauffeur steps out and opens the door as if he expects you to get in.

What will you do now?
If you get into the car,
turn to **page 27.**

If you are suspicious and
decide to take the next
bus to Uncle Herbert's
house, turn to **page 33.**

24   You take the lifeboat and head back for Bonesboro.

It is very dark. Rain is pouring down. The *Scull and Bones* is lost from sight. You pick up the oars and start rowing. But you are lost. Leaving the boat may have been a big mistake.

Go on to the next page.

There is a flash of lightning. You think you see the sail of another boat not far away.

More lightning. Yes! The sail is coming closer!

"HELP!" you shout.

Now you can see the sail more clearly.

OOPS! It is not a sail. It is a fin — A BIG FIN.

Turn to **page 26.**

26 You paddle as fast as you can. But the shark is right behind you. You'd better put on some speed or this could be . . .

THE END

You get into the car.

The driver takes you to a part of town you've never seen before.

You stop in front of a big house. The address is 14 China Court.

"Go inside," says the driver. "Someone is expecting you."

In the living room, sitting in a big chair is . . .

Turn to page 28.

Uncle Herbert!

You cannot believe your eyes.

"I . . . I . . . I thought you were dead," you stammer.

Uncle Herbert laughs. "Heh, heh, heh! As you can see, I'm quite alive."

"But what about your will?" you ask.

"I just pretended to be dead to see how far my greedy relatives would go to get my diamond. But none of you are going to have it. The Dandee Diamond is staying with the one who deserves it most — ME!!!"

THE END

You have found the diamond!

But who does it really belong to?

You see a note wrapped around Arthur's leg. Arthur is not too happy about letting you have the note, but you manage to get it off without being bitten.

What does the note say?

Flip a coin.
Is it heads?
Then turn to **page 50.**

Is it tails?
Then turn to **page 56.**

You all run until you reach the water-front.

Drusilla hails a passing water taxi and makes a flying leap for it. As she jumps, the diamond slips out of her hand.

Captain Jack lunges for it. He's got it!

OOPS! The dock is very slippery. You start to fall. You bump into Captain Jack.

The diamond flies up into the air.

Drusilla, Captain Jack, and you all grab for it.

Turn to **page 41.**

You decide to forget about Doubloon Island and stay on the boat with Captain Jack. Two weeks later you arrive in Hong Kong.

"What do we do now?" you ask. "China is an awfully big place."

"Our first stop is right here in Hong Kong," Captain Jack says, "at the China Dragon Tea House. Your uncle and I drank many a cup of tea there in our younger days. That's where Herb won the diamond from Professor Dandee."

Turn to **page 32.**

32 You go to the China Dragon Tea House and order lunch.

There is something strange about your waitress. All the other waitresses are small and delicate. Yours is almost six feet tall and is wearing a lot of makeup. When you came in she was sitting at a corner table drinking tea. You noticed that Captain Jack gave her a long hard look, as if he'd seen her before.

Turn to **page 38.**

You take the next bus to Uncle Herbert's house and find Roderick busily digging up the backyard.

*If you decide to hide
and watch what happens,
turn to* **page 37.**

*If you decide to let
him know you are here,
turn to* **page 46.**

Captain Jack grabs the cookie and cracks it open. The Dandee Diamond falls into his hand.

"Let's get out of here," he shouts. He runs out of the tea house with you right behind him.

You both race back to the *Scull and Bones*. But when you get there, you see something is very wrong. What used to be the boat is now a smoldering heap of burnt wood and canvas.

"This looks like Drusilla's work," says Jack.

Go on to the next page.

"What do we do now?" you ask.

"Get to the airport and back to Bonesboro as fast as we can," he replies.

At the airport you hire a private plane to take you back to Bonesboro. Once you are in the air, Captain Jack breathes a sigh of relief.

"Everything will be fine now," he says. "We'll sell the diamond and both be millionaires."

Suddenly the plane starts flying upside down and doing wild loop-the-loops.

What's wrong?

You both run to the cockpit.

The pilot turns and smiles.

Turn to **page 36.**

36   It's Drusilla!

"You are in my hands now," she crows.

"That's what you think," says Captain Jack. "Back at the tea house I slipped a sleeping potion into your tea. It should take effect just about now!"

Drusilla slumps forward. She is out like a light.

Captain Jack takes the controls. "Bet you didn't know I could fly a plane, too," he says with a wink.

You fly back to Bonesboro, the Dandee Diamond yours at last. Soon you and Captain Jack will both be millionaires.

THE END

You hide and watch Roderick as he digs a deeper and deeper hole. He has found something! But why does he look so mad?

You see Roderick throw down his shovel in disgust and stalk off. As soon as he is gone, you run over to the hole. On the ground is — a playing card. The ace of diamonds!

No wonder Roderick was mad. It looks like this is another one of Uncle Herbert's jokes.

Or is it?

If you decide to give up the search, too, turn to **page 52.**

If you want to stick around and keep looking, turn to **page 40.**

38   When you are finished with your meal, the owner of the tea house comes to your table carrying a plate with one gigantic fortune cookie on it.

"Are you the party that is looking for the Dandee Diamond?" he asks.

You and Captain Jack nod. Your waitress looks very interested.

"Mr. Bone left this here for you," says the owner.

You both reach for the fortune cookie. So does the waitress.

Oh-oh! You've seen those long red fingernails before. They belong to Drusilla Devine!

Who gets the cookie?
If Drusilla does,
turn to **page 42.**

If Captain Jack does,
turn to **page 34.**

If you do, turn to **page 44.**

40　　You stay in Uncle Herbert's yard and keep looking for clues.

You have just about run out of ideas when you notice a beautiful rosebush covered with tiny red roses. A little sign planted in the ground in front of it says: BONE'S FAMOUS CHINA TEA ROSES.

You remember the parrot's words: "China, China . . . look in China . . ." You begin digging furiously.

You strike something hard. The diamond?

It is!

Lying beside the diamond is—another letter! You open it and read Uncle Herbert's last message. It says:

Congratulations!
You stuck with the search and so you deserve to keep the Dandee Diamond
How does it feel to be rich?
　　　　Love,
　　　　Herbert J. Bone, Esquire

THE END

But you all miss.

You can't believe it! You are watching the fabulous Dandee Diamond sink to the bottom of the South China Sea!

THE END

Drusilla snatches the cookie and cracks it open.

The Dandee Diamond falls into her hand.

"It's mine—all mine," she laughs, and runs out of the tea house.

Captain Jack runs after her and so do you. The chase is on!

Go on to the next page.

The three of you race through the narrow streets of Hong Kong. Soon you

run smack into a parade for the Chinese New Year. Firecrackers are popping all around you, and a long, dancing "dragon" with 20 people inside is coming down the street. Drusilla darts in front of it. You've lost her!

"There she is!" shouts Captain Jack, pointing. "She is heading for the docks."

Turn to **page 30.**

44   You snatch the cookie.

"Give it back," screams Drusilla.

"Come on," you shout to Captain Jack. "Let's get out of here."

"Not so fast," says Captain Jack, pulling a gun from his pocket.

"But I thought you were my friend," you say.

"You thought wrong," replies Captain Jack. "Give me that cookie."

Go on to the next page.

You knock the table over on Captain Jack and Drusilla and race outside.

As soon as you are safe, you crack open the cookie and read the fortune inside:

LO OKIN ART HUR SCAGE

It must be a clue! Maybe the words are broken in the wrong places.

Can you solve the puzzle?
If you can,
turn to **page 51.**

46   You can't wait to tell Roderick what you think of him. You run up to him yelling, "You dirty double-crosser!"

Roderick looks up and sniffs. "I should have let you come with me. This digging is hard work. Want to help?"

You say, "Are you kidding? Now it's every man for himself."

Two hours later you are both still digging. Roderick looks as if he's ready to call it quits. Then suddenly his face is all smiles. He has found something — a fancy leather box.

Inside is a jewel the size of an egg, sparkling so much that you almost need sunglasses to look at it. The Dandee Diamond! Oh, no!

"Finders keepers," Roderick sneers, as he pockets the diamond and takes off. "And losers you-know-what!"

What a rotten deal. That no-good Roderick has all the luck. You are about to leave when you see a letter. It is from Uncle Herbert. Who else?

Turn to **page 48.**

You open the letter. It says:

Well, you found it.
I guess I can let you know now
that the fabulous Dandee Diamond
is really just a fabulous fake.
You are now the proud owner of the
world's largest rhinestone!
            Love,
            Herbert J. Bone, Esquire

You smile to yourself. Roderick hasn't had the last laugh after all. Uncle Herbert has!

THE END

50 The coin came up heads. You read the message. It says:

You guessed it. Arthur is the best friend I ever had. He deserves my diamond. Now he is the richest parrot in the world!

Herbert J. Bone, Esquire

PS. Good luck to you, too.

THE END

Yes, that's what the clue means.

Oh, boy! You've come all the way to Hong Kong for nothing.

You wire your parents for money and catch the next plane home to Bonesboro. As soon as you arrive, you head straight for Uncle Herbert's house and go to Arthur the parrot's room.

Turn to **page 17.**

You decide to give up the search. You are tired and hungry.

On your way home, you pass the local Burpee Burger. "Go in, go in," your empty stomach growls.

As you step inside, sirens go off and lights flash. Burpee the Clown runs up in his clodhopper shoes and shakes your hand.

Go on to the next page.

"Great jumping Burpee Burgers!" he cries. "You are our one-zillionth customer, and you have just won one million dollars and a lifetime supply of Burpee Burgers!"

WOW! A million dollars and all the Burpee Burgers you can eat. Who cares about Uncle Herbert and his old diamond now? You are rich!

THE END

54 You wade ashore and take a look at your new home.

There is plenty of fruit and coconuts for you to eat. But there are a lot of things that Doubloon Island doesn't have . . . like people, for instance. You hunt for any signs of life but all you find is a large and rather shaggy monkey.

He seems very gentle and eager to be friends. That's fine with you. This is no time to be choosy.

You name your new buddy Ernest. You teach him how to play catch with a coconut, and he shows you how to swing from trees.

One day you and Ernest are on the beach building a sand castle.

Suddenly Ernest starts screeching, "Cheep! Cheep! Cheep!" He has found something buried in the sand!

You dig deeper. It is a chest . . . old Peg Leg's treasure chest!

Go on to the next page.

The chest is filled with gold coins and jewels. You and Ernest are rich . . . richer than Uncle Herbert ever dreamed of being.

But the two of you have nowhere to spend your money. If only a ship would sail by and rescue you. But that's a big if . . .

THE END

56   The coin came up tails. The note says:

Congratulations!
You figured out all the clues so
you deserve the diamond.
Herbert J. Bone, Esquire

PS. I am also leaving you my parrot,
Arthur. Since you are rich now, I
know you'll keep him in the style to
which he has become accustomed.

THE END